Lexile Level:

_____

Award/Other:

_____

SHORT TALES

GREEK MYTHS

MEDUSA

Adapted by Rob M. Worley
Illustrated by Mike Dubisch

GREEN LEVEL	BLUE LEVEL	PINK LEVEL
• Familiar topics	• New ideas introduced	• More complex ideas
• Frequently used words	• Larger vocabulary	• Extended vocabulary
• Repeating language patterns	• Variety of language patterns	• Expanded sentence structures

To learn more about Short Tales leveling, go to www.abdopublishing.com

Published by Magic Wagon, a division of the ABDO Publishing Group, 8000 West 78th Street, Edina, Minnesota, 55439. Copyright © 2008 by Abdo Consulting Group, Inc. International copyrights reserved in all countries. All rights reserved. No part of this book may be reproduced in any form without written permission from the publisher. Short Tales ™ is a trademark and logo of Magic Wagon.

Printed in the United States.

Adapted Text by Rob M. Worley
Illustrations by Mike Dubisch
Colors by Jeremy Shepherd
Edited by Stephanie Hedlund
Interior Layout by Kristen Fitzner Denton
Book Design and Packaging by Shannon Eric Denton

Library of Congress Cataloging-in-Publication Data
Worley, Rob M.
  Medusa / adapted by Rob M. Worley ; illustrated by Mike Dubisch.
    p. cm. -- (Short tales Greek myths)
  ISBN 978-1-60270-137-3
  1. Medusa (Greek mythology)--Juvenile literature. I. Dubisch, Michael.
II. Title.
BL820.M38W67 2008
398.20938'01--dc22
                        2007036093

THE GREEK GODS

ZEUS:
Ruler of Gods
& Men

ATHENA:
Goddess of
Wisdom

HEPHAESTUS:
God of Fire
& Metalworking

HERA:
Goddess of Marriage
Queen of the Gods

HERMES:
Messenger of
the Gods

HESTIA:
Goddess of the
Hearth & Home

POSEIDON:
God of the Sea

APHRODITE:
Goddess of Love

ARES:
God of War

ARTEMIS:
Goddess of
the Hunt

APOLLO:
God of the Sun

HADES:
God of the
Underworld

Mythical Beginning

Medusa appears in many Greek myths. She is usually shown as a snake-haired monster. In many stories Medusa was born a monster. She and her three sisters were called the Gorgons.

Other stories say Medusa was born a beautiful sea nymph. Her vanity angered the goddess Athena. So, Athena transformed her into a monster.

Ceto was a horrible sea monster.

Men and fish alike feared her.

She swam the oceans for hundreds of years.

"I'm so ugly no one can love me," Ceto said.

One day she met Phorcys.

Phorcys was a horrible sea monster, too.

They fell in love at once.

Ceto had a baby.

She and Phorcys expected it to be a hideous monster.

So true was their love for each other that the baby was born beautiful.

Her name was Medusa.

Ceto and Phorcys often told Medusa she was beautiful.

When she grew into a woman Medusa said, "I am too pretty to live with you horrible monsters."

It broke their monstrous hearts.

Medusa moved to the beautiful city of Athens.

The goddess Athena watched over the city.

"I am even more beautiful than Athena," Medusa declared to all who would listen.

A few men believed it.

The ocean god Poseidon took notice of Medusa.

"She is quite beautiful," he told Athena. "I think she may even be more beautiful than you."

This made Athena angry.

One day Athena visited Medusa.

"You are not so beautiful," Athena said. "You hurt your parents terribly. On the inside you are very ugly."

"It is only outer beauty that matters," said Medusa.

"You are wrong," Athena said. "Your cruelty turns every heart to stone."

Then Athena said, "I will make your outsides match what's inside."

Athena used her godly powers to transform Medusa.

Medusa's white teeth turned to jagged fangs.

Her lovely hands turned to horrible claws.

Medusa's beautiful hair became a nest of hissing snakes.

"Now you are as ugly on the outside as you are on the inside," Athena said.

"You'll turn more than hearts to stone," Athena said.

Soon, a man came looking for the beautiful Medusa.

He found a monster instead.

When he looked into her eyes, he was transformed into a stone statue.

Medusa fled the city and found a cave to live in.

Everyone said she was a monster.

She believed it.

Athena appeared to Medusa.

"When you find true beauty inside you, your appearance won't matter," Athena said.

This made Medusa angry.

"You have taken all my beauty from me," Medusa said.

"I do not believe in inner beauty," Medusa said. "I will be the monster you have made me."

So, Medusa terrorized everyone.

Men came to stop her.

But, they were all turned to stone.

Across the sea, King Polydectes heard about Medusa's terrible powers.

He decided to send a promising hero to defeat her.

Polydectes visited young Perseus. Perseus was the son of Zeus.

"If you slay Medusa you will be the greatest hero of all time," Polydectes said.

He forgot to tell Perseus that Medusa could turn him to stone.

To learn more about Medusa, Perseus visited the Old Gray Women.

They were Medusa's sisters.

They had only one eye between them.

They had to pass the eye around to take turns seeing with it.

They would not tell Perseus where to find Medusa.

So, he snatched their eye away from them.

"Tell me and I'll give you your eye back," he said.

The Old Gray Women were desperate to get their eye.

They gave Perseus winged sandals that would carry him to Medusa.

They also gave him a helmet that made him invisible.

But, they secretly hoped Medusa would turn him to stone.

Athena met Perseus as he arrived near Medusa's cave.

She gave him a shield polished so smooth it became a mirror.

"Polydectes has not told you everything," Athena said. "Do not look directly at Medusa."

Perseus entered Medusa's cave with his weapons.

Even as he hunted her, she hunted him.

Medusa tried to turn him to stone like everyone else.

But, Perseus used the shield and only looked at her reflection.

He never looked at her face.

Perseus waited until Medusa fell asleep. Then, he put on his helmet.

While invisible, he snuck up on Medusa and struck her with his sword.

He had defeated the monster.

Perseus took pity on Medusa.

He buried her body.

He saved some of her blood for Athena.

Then, Perseus placed Medusa's head in a bag so that it could not turn anyone else to stone.

Then something amazing happened.

Medusa's blood mixed with the earth and formed clay.

The clay took shape on its own.

It came to life as a winged horse!

Perseus named the horse Pegasus.

He was amazed such beauty had been inside such an ugly creature.

Medusa had beauty inside her after all.

Her blood was special.

Athena would even use it to cure the sick.